W9-ALJ-782

Shoe Print Art

Step into Drawing

Create 55 shoe print drawings
step by step!

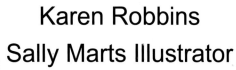

Karen Robbins

Sally Marts Illustrator

Hide & Seek Press

Attention schools and businesses: Bulk purchases for educational, business and
organizations are available from Hide & Seek Press. Please contact the publisher.

Photographs by Millie Herd, Sally Marts, Barbara Clark,
Marji Overgaard, Jean Best, Derek Boucher, Karen Robbins.

First Printing: Printed in China
ISBN 978-0-9711441-1-8

Publisher's Cataloging-in-Publication
(Provided by Quality Books, Inc.)
Robbins, Karen, 1944-
Shoe print art : step into drawing : create 55 shoe
print drawings : step by step! / Karen Robbins ; Sally
Marts, Illustrator.
p. cm.
SUMMARY : Shows fifty-five shoe print images with
simple steps on how to draw monsters, dinosaurs,
animals, holiday characters and transportation vehicles.
Audience: Ages 4-14.
ISBN 978-0-9711441-1-8
1. Drawing--Technique--Juvenile literature.
[1.Drawing.] I.Marts, Sally, ill. II. Title.
NC655.R63 2012 741.2
 QBII2-600116

Edited by MaryAnn F. Kohl

This book is dedicated to all the doodlers in the world who aspire to become artists.

My deepest thank you to Sally Marts, my talented, graphic designer. Sally "magically" transformed my doodles and added many more of her own designs to create this beautiful beginning drawing book for children. She is an amazing, gifted artist and a joy to work with. Special thanks to MaryAnn Kohl of Bright Ring Publishing, who graciously gave of her time and expertise in guiding me step by step creating Shoe Print ART. MaryAnn is one of the leading experts in ART for Early Childhood Education, and is a popular presenter at conferences across America.

Thanks to all the children who drew an image for my Shoe Print ART book. They worked like professional artists using their creativity to do their very best work! I am so proud of them. What creative, talented beginning artists! Lastly, I am grateful to the children's parents, their grandmothers, and my friends who helped coordinate and assist the children with their drawings. A world of thanks to each of you!

Karen

Dear Artists

I love art and I love to draw! But beginning to learn to draw takes lots of practice. For over twenty years, I've taught Shoe Print Art to kids and teachers. I discovered anyone can draw almost anything from a shoe print!

So, grab a piece of white paper and a pencil. Trace the plain shoe print sample at the back of this book, and step into drawing step by step. After drawing the plain shoe print with a pencil, choose one drawing and follow the steps. When completed, color with crayons, colored pencils, or paint. Use your own creativity to enhance your drawing.

If the kids in my book can do it, you can too! I arranged the drawings by level of difficulty. The easiest images are in the front and gradually become more difficult. So, start with the first one and keep drawing until you complete all 55 ideas. Then, use your imagination and creativity to create your very own drawings.

You'll find groups of various themes or categories throughout the book. You can also turn your creations into greeting cards, note cards or even foam refrigerator magnets.

Hope you have hours of fun drawing from shoe prints! Step into drawing step by step! You'll be on your way becoming an artist!

Creatively,
Karen Robbins

Table of Contents

3 Dedication
4 Letter from Karen
5 Table of Contents
6 Balloon
7 Ghost
8 Mummy
9 Bat
10 Spider
11 Butterfly
12 Ladybug
13 Bumblebee
14 Wing Monster
15 Shape Monster
16 King Monster
17 Triceratops
18 Brachiosaurus
19 Tyrannosaurus Rex

20 Rabbit
21 Rooster
22 Chick
23 Parrot
24 Owl
25 Mouse
26 Pig
27 Dog
28 Cat
29 Puppy
30 Lion
31 Panda
32 Monkey
33 Giraffe
34 Gecko
35 Alligator
36 Frog

37 Gum Ball Machine
38 Airplane
39 Helicopter
40 Rocket Ship
41 Race Car
42 Submarine
43 Shark
44 Crab
45 Turtle
46 Seal
47 Octopus
48 Swordfish
49 Seahorse
50 Lobster
51 Mermaid
52 Pirate
53 Clown

54 Fairy
55 Witch
56 Turkey
57 Reindeer
58 Santa
59 Snowman
60 Penguin
61 Artists at Work
62 Original Creations
   by Young Artists
63 Magnets & Greeting Cards
64 Small Multiple Shoe
   Print Creations
65 Shoe Message
66 Shoe Print Template
67 Letter from Soles 4 Souls
68 Contact Information

Balloon

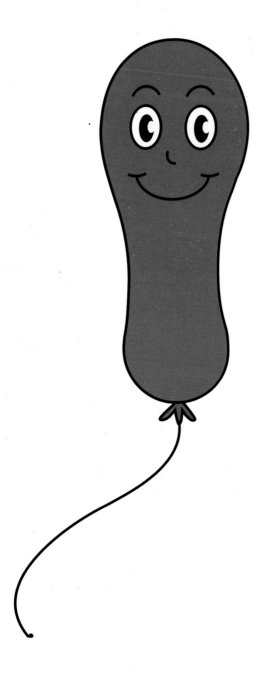

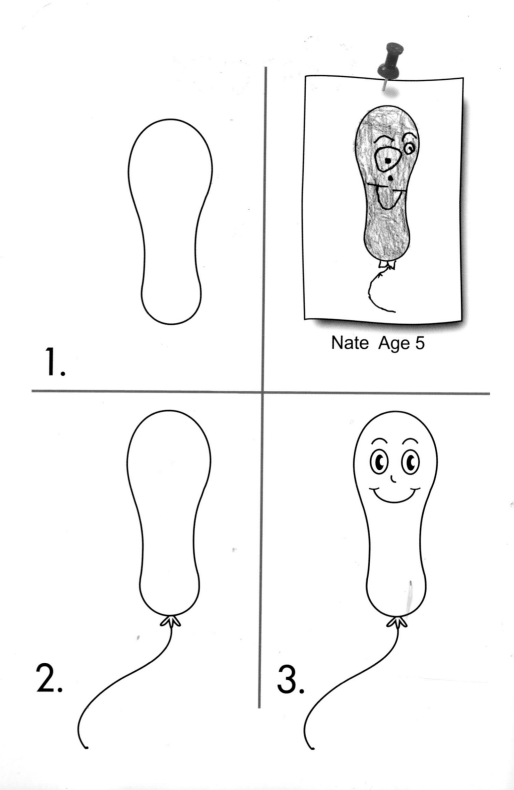

Nate Age 5

1.

2.

3.

6

Ghost

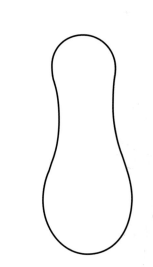

1.

Juliana Age 3

2.

3.

7

Mummy

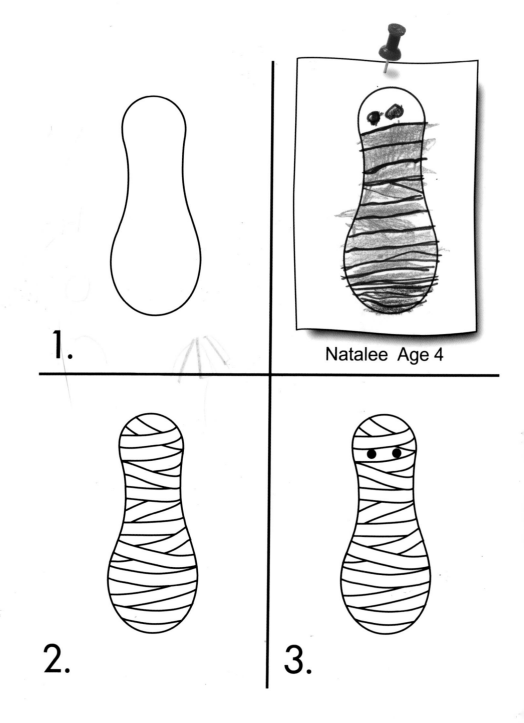

1.

Natalee Age 4

2.

3.

Bat

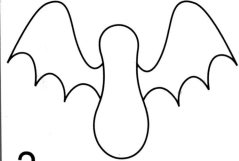

Jeffrey Age 6

1.

2.

3.

4.

Spider

Grant Age 8

1.

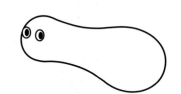

2.

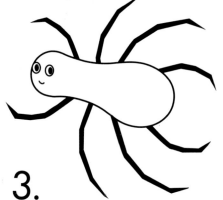

3.

4.

Butterfly

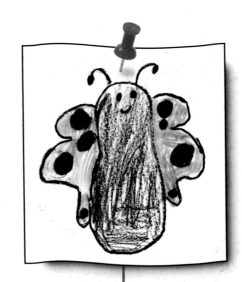

1.

2.

3.

4.

11

Ladybug

1.

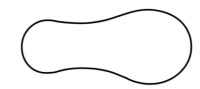

Claire K. Age 8

2.

3.

4.

5.

12

Bumblebee

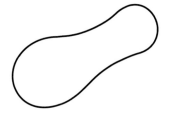
1.

Mason Age 7

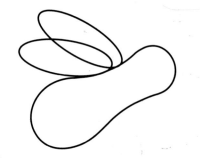
2.

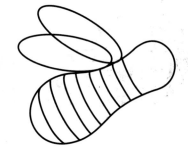
3.

4.

5.

Wing Monster

1.

2.

Sophia Age 6

3.

4.

5.

14

Shape Monster

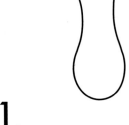

1.

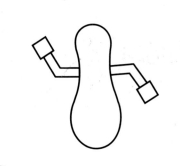

2.

Hannah Age 6

3.

4.

5.

15

King Monster

1.

2.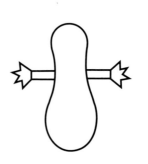

3.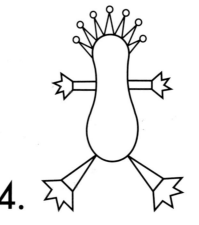

Taylor Age 4

4.

5.

16

Triceratops

Coleman Age 6

1.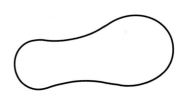

2.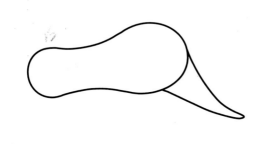

3.

4.

17

Brachiosaurus

Dylan Age 6

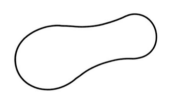

1.

2.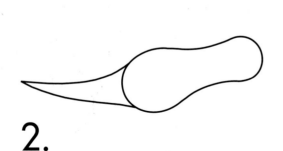

3.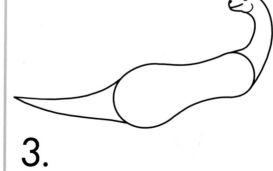

4.

18

Tyrannosaurus Rex

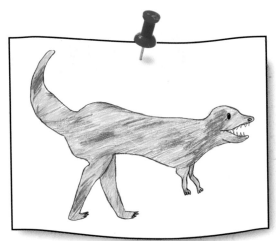

Cade Age 9

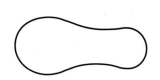

1.

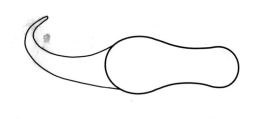

2.

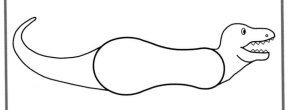

3.

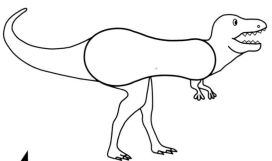

4.

Rabbit

1.

2.

3.

Madelyne Age 7

4.

5.

Rooster

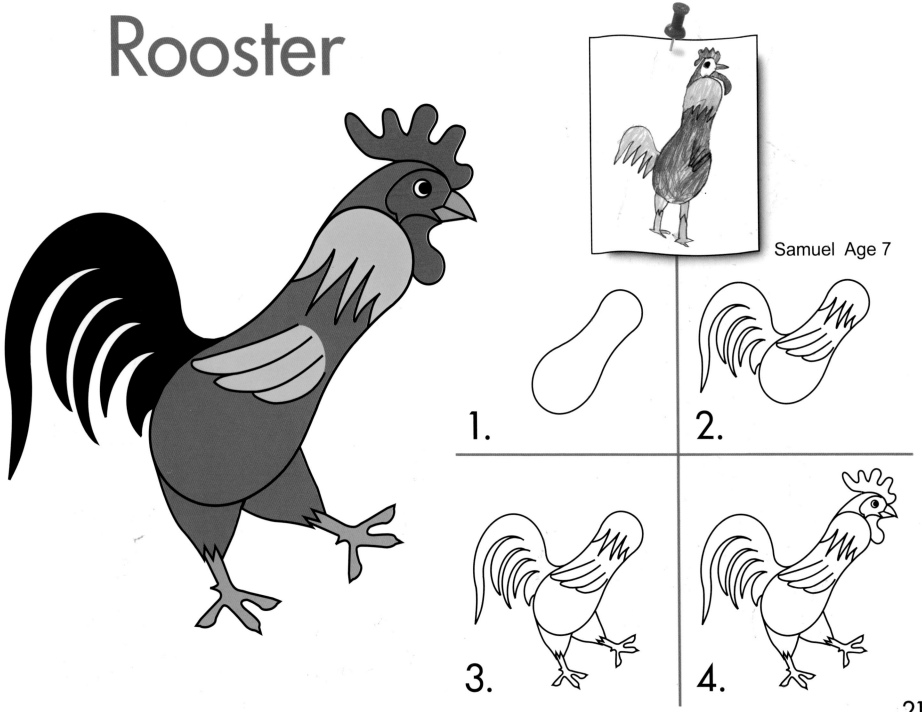

Samuel Age 7

1.

2.

3.

4.

21

Chick

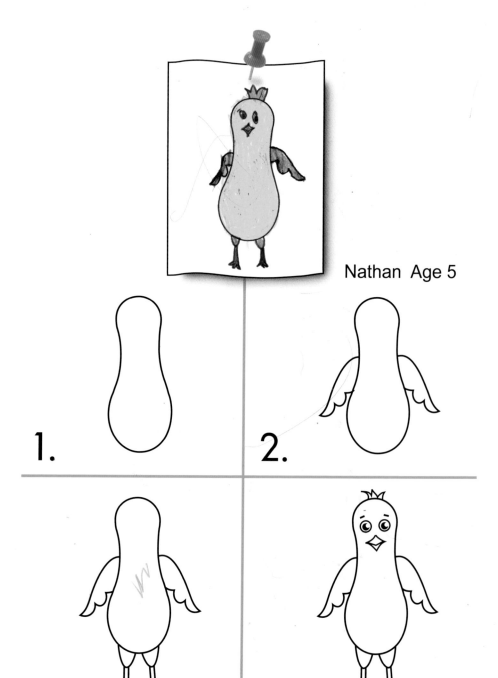

Nathan Age 5

1.

2.

3.

4.

Parrot

Marlo Age 5

1.

2.

3.

4.

Owl

1.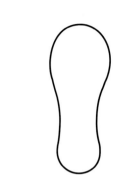

Luke Age 12

2.

3.

4.

5.

24

Mouse

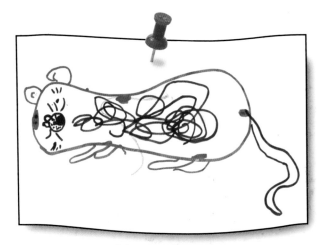

Alana Age 4

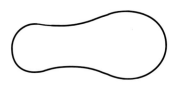
1.

2.

3.

4.

25

Pig

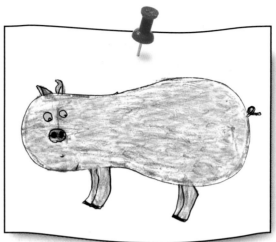

Josh Age 6

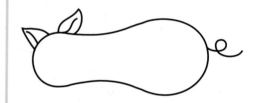

1.

2.

3.

4.

Dog

Ash Age 8½

1.

2.

3.

4.

5.

27

Cat

1.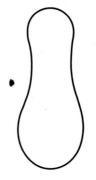

Macey Age 9

2.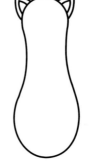

3.

4.

5.

Puppy

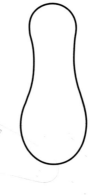

1.

Brooke Age 9

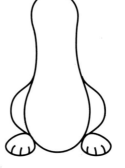

2.

3.

4.

5.

Lion

Hannah Age 6

1.

2.

3.

4.

5.

30

Panda

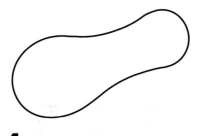

1.

Chloe Age 10

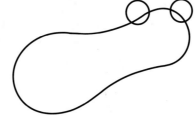

2.

3.

4.

5.

31

Monkey

Madison Age 13

1.

2.

3.

4.

5.

Giraffe

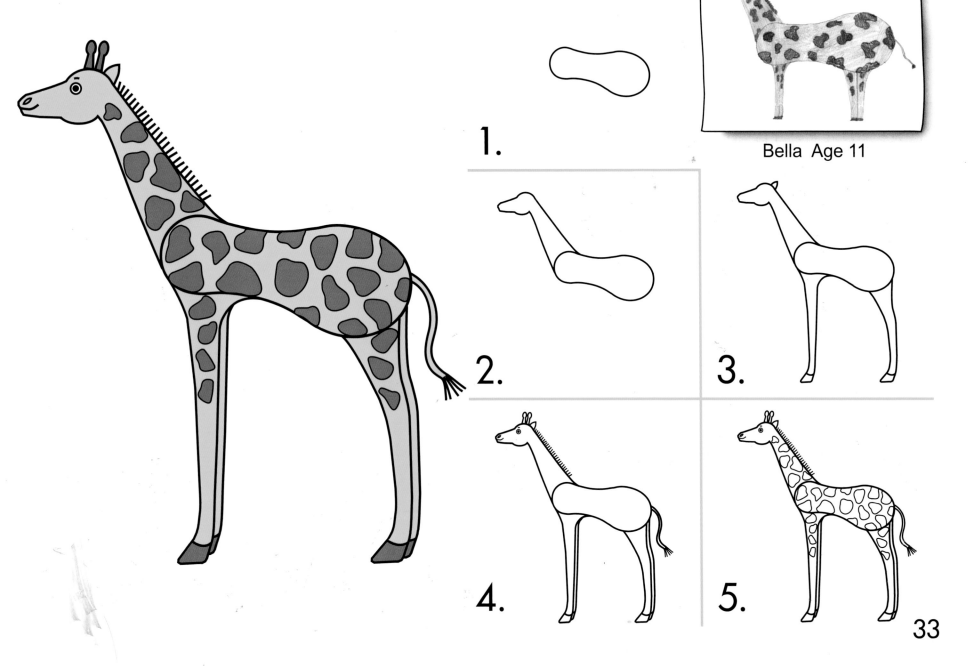

1.

2.

3.

4.

5.

Bella Age 11

33

Gecko

Claire W. Age 8

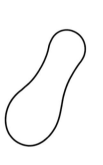

1.

2.

3.

4.

34

Alligator

Lillian Age 8

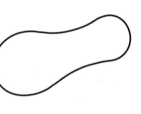

1.

2.

3.

4.

35

Frog

Trevor Age 12

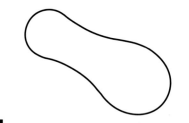

1.

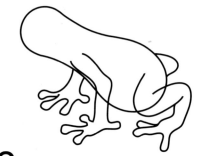

2.

3.

4.

5.

Gum Ball Machine

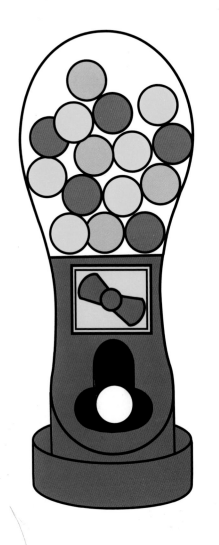

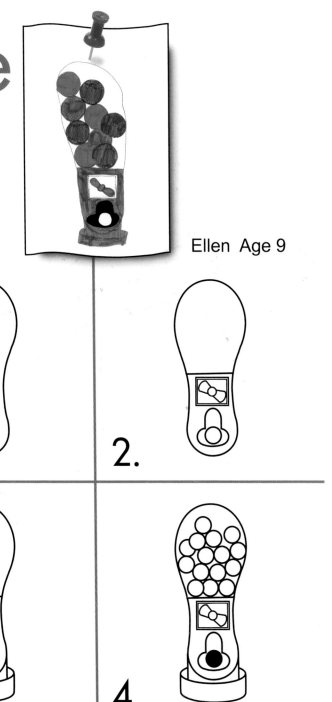

Ellen Age 9

1.

2.

3.

4.

37

Airplane

Allison Age 6

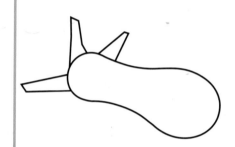

1.

2.

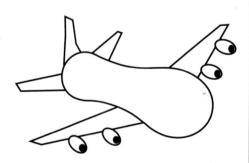

3.

4.

38

Helicopter

Ryker Age 8

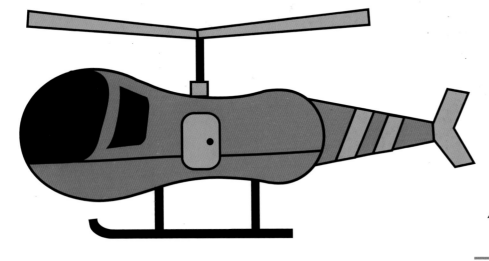

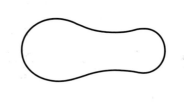

1.

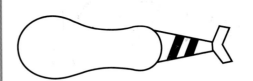

2.

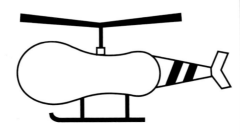

3.

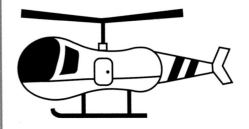

4.

Rocket Ship

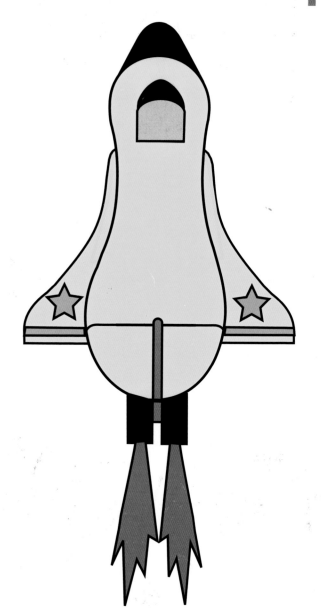

1.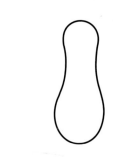

2.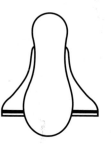

3.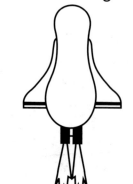

Caleb P. Age 9

4.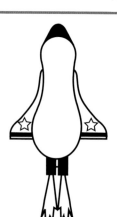

5.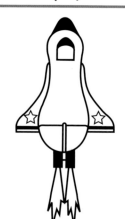

Race Car

Brydan Age 9

1.

2.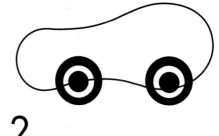

3.

4.

Submarine

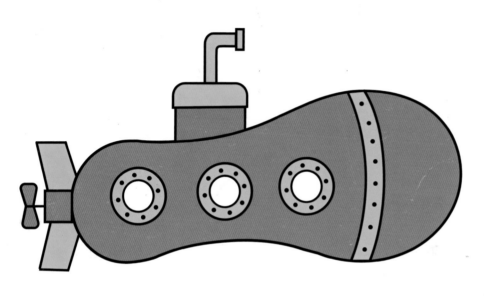

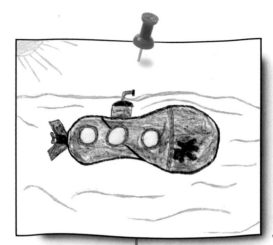

Jesse Age 9

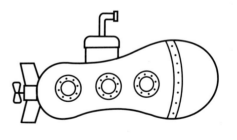

1.

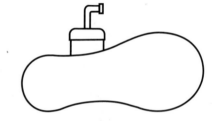

2.

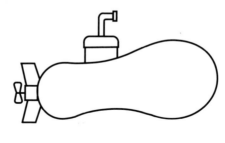

3.

4.

42

Shark

Tommy Age 9

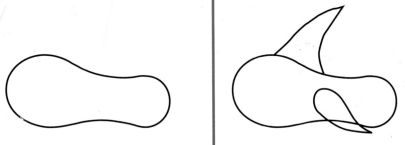

1.

2.

3.

4.

Crab

Alexandra Age 6

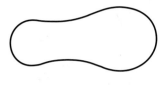

1.

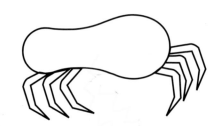

2.

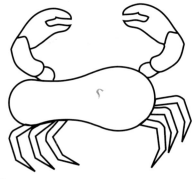

3.

4.

Turtle

Annika Age 9

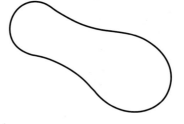

1.

2.

3.

4.

45

Seal

Lily Age 8

1.

2.

3.

4.

46

Octopus

Mimi Age 10

1.

2.

3.

4.

Swordfish

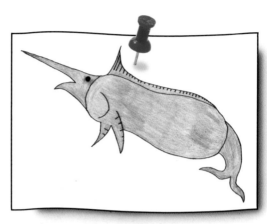

Ryan Age 8

1.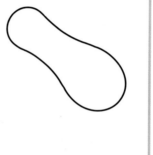

2.

3.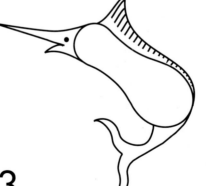

4.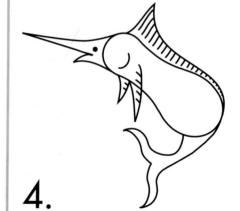

Seahorse

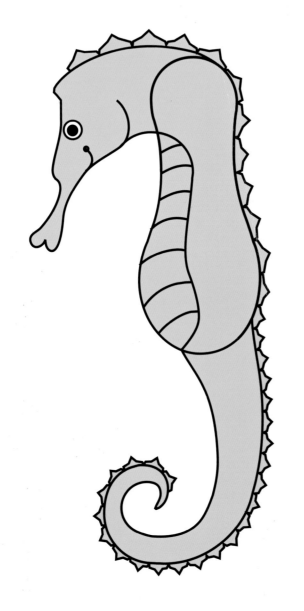

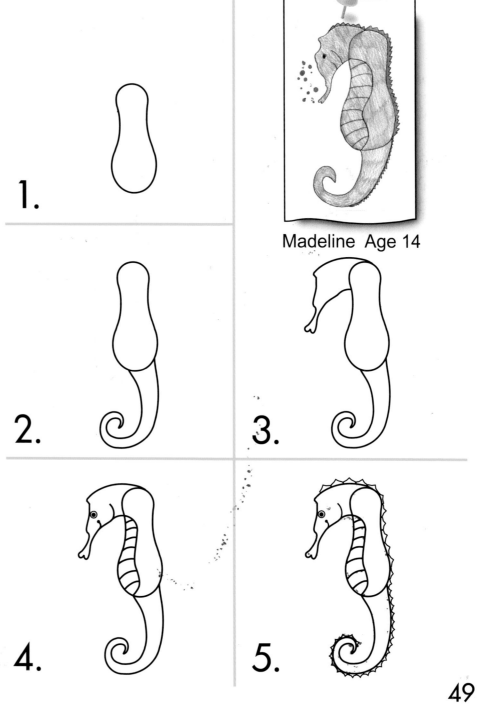

Madeline Age 14

1.

2.

3.

4.

5.

49

Lobster

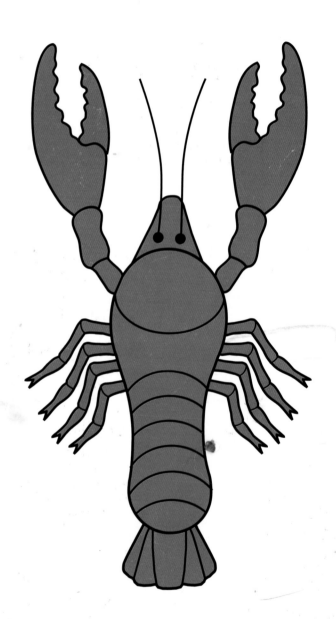

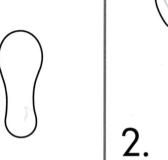

Belle Age 10

1.

2.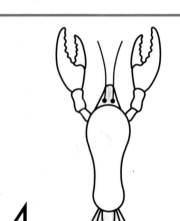

3.

4.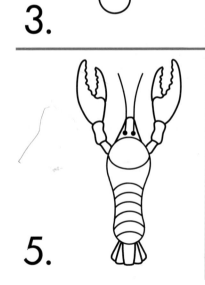

5.

6.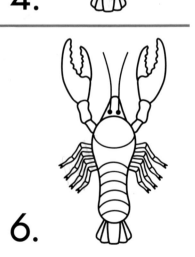

50

Mermaid

Samantha Age 10

1.

2.

3.

4.

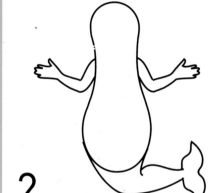

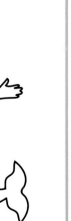

Pirate

John Age 10

1.

2.

3.

4.

5.

6.

Clown

1.

Ashley Age 12

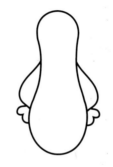
2.

3.

4.

5.

Fairy

Avery Age 6

1.

2.

3.

4.

5.

6.

Witch

1.

2.

3.

4.

5.

Grace Age 7

55

Turkey

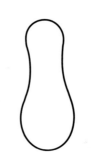

1.

Isla Age 7

2.

3.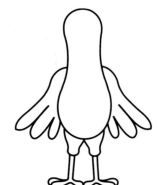

4.

5.

56

Reindeer

Bayden Age 5

1.

2.
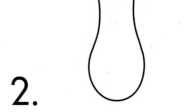

3.

4.

57

Santa

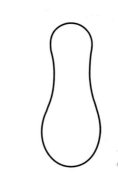

1.

Emma Age 13

2.

3.

4.

5.

58

Snowman

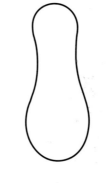
1.

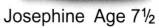
Josephine Age 7½

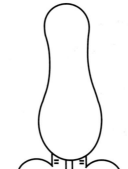
2.

3.

4.

5.

Penguin

1.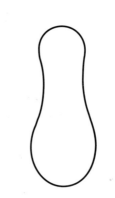

2.

3.

4.

5.

Kate Age 12

Artists at Work

Kira Age 4½

LOVEY

Meg Age 4

aff woof wee!

Jane Age 8

Caleb Age 9

Peter Age 6

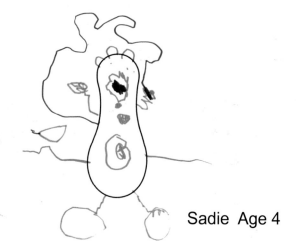

Sadie Age 4

Isla Age 7

Jesse Age 9

62

Foam Magnets

Hey kids, how would you like to make a shoe print foam refrigerator magnet? They're fun, quick and easy. Here's how. Using white paper, draw and cut patterns, and then trace the parts on the back side of colored foam. Carefully cut out the pieces and glue the parts on with craft glue. Or, purchase colored foam with the adhesive backing. Just cut, peel and stick. Take two adhesive backed magnet pieces and peel and stick to the back of the foam shoe print image. Your refrigerator magnet is ready to hold pictures and messages. How cute! Why not make another one, and give as a gift!

Greeting Cards

Would you like to make your very own hand made greeting card? Here's how. First choose an envelope and then take a piece of construction paper and cut to fit. Now fold your paper in half. Decide if you want to make it vertical or horizontal. This will be determined by the image you choose. Select the shoe print image and draw step by step with a pencil. Finish with crayons or colored pencils. Or you can also cut parts from colored construction paper and paste onto the front of the folded card. Carefully write your message inside. Wow! You're a card designer! What fun! Your family and friends will be thrilled to receive a handcrafted shoe print card made by you!

63

Small Multiple Shoe Print Creations

Putting your best foot forward,
you can draw anything!
Have fun drawing!

Karen and Sally

Shoe Print Template

To make the drawings inside, place a piece of white paper over the page and trace over the larger shoe pattern with a pencil. Follow each step one at a time using your pencil. To finish, add your own creactivity using crayons, colored pencils or paint. The smaller pattern is for refrigerator magnets and smaller shoeprint creations. Trace the shoe print pattern onto a piece of white paper and then cut out to make a pattern. Trace around the pattern on the back side of foam or construction paper.   Karen and Sally

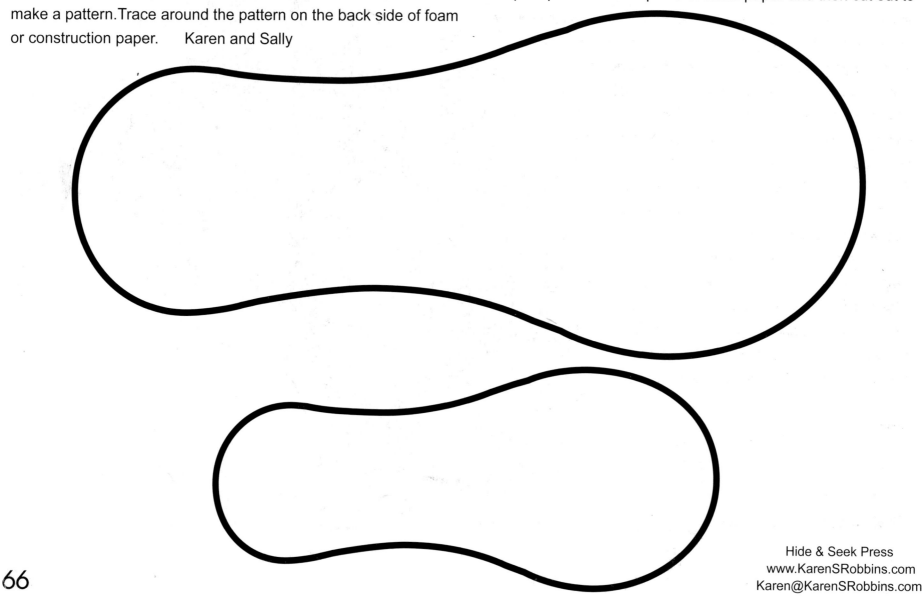

Hide & Seek Press
www.KarenSRobbins.com
Karen@KarenSRobbins.com

Everyday around the world there are millions of children that have to walk barefoot. During those walks, they are at risk of diseases like hookworm or Mossy Foot. In fact, they are more likely to suffer from hookworm in countries like Haiti and Tanzania than from any other disease. And a simple pair of shoes can protect them and keep them healthy and happy. Which, here at Soles4Souls, is exactly what we want—happy children! With the purchase of this book, you are partnering with Soles4Souls to help put shoes on the feet of kids who cannot afford them. For around $1, Soles4Souls can send a pair of shoes to kids who are barefoot. So, as you're tracing the outline of your shoe to turn it into a fun piece of art, remember that you're also helping millions around the world receive their first pair of shoes. Thank you so much for your support and be sure to check out all that we are doing at Soles4Souls to help people by visiting www.giveshoes.org.

Sincerely,

Paul Wilson

Co-Founder of Soles4Souls

Contact Information

Please contact Karen Robbins to arrange for an in service teacher training workshop, conference presenter, or to teach a shoe print art demonstration/class. For over twenty years, Karen has taught shoe print art to children and teachers. It's been rewarding to see children and adults successfully draw from a shoe print shape by following simple steps. I've been amazed at their finished works of art.

For further information or to purchase large quantities of *Shoe Print Art*, please contact Karen Robbins of Hide & Seek Press. And remember, putting your best foot forward, you can draw anything! Have fun drawing!

Attention: schools, businesses, and organizations. *Shoe Print Art* is available for quantity discounts with bulk purchases for educational, business, or sales promotion use. Please contact Hide & Seek Press.

I am pleased to give a percentage of the sales from *Shoe Print Art* to Soles 4 Souls. I hope you will support them too. Together, we can begin to "change the world one pair at a time!"

Karen Robbins, Publisher

Hide and Seek Press
www.KarenSRobbins.com
Karen@KarenSRobbins.com